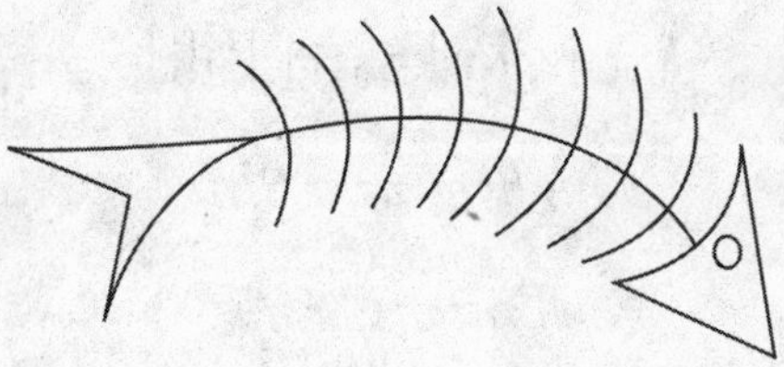

Also by Kirkpatrick Hill:

*Toughboy and Sister*

*Winter Camp*

# The Year of
# Miss Agnes

## Kirkpatrick Hill

Margaret K. McElderry Books
NEW YORK · LONDON · TORONTO · SYDNEY · SINGAPORE

Margaret K. McElderry Books
An imprint of the Simon & Schuster Children's Publishing Division
1230 Avenue of the Americas, New York, NY 10020

Book design by David Caplan
The text of this book is set in Adobe Caslon.
Printed in the United States of America
2 4 6 8 10 9 7 5 3 1
Library of Congress Cataloging-in-Publication Data
Hill, Kirkpatrick.
The year of Miss Agnes / Kirkpatrick Hill.   p.   cm.
Summary: Ten-year-old Fred (short for Frederika) narrates the story of
school and village life among the Athabascans in Alaska during 1948
when Miss Agnes arrived as the new teacher.
ISBN 0-689-82933-7
[1. Schools—Fiction. 2. Teachers—Fiction.
3. Athapascan Indians—Fiction. 4. Indians of North
America—Alaska—Fiction. 5. Alaska—Fiction.] I. Title.
PZ7.H55285  Ye2000  [Fic]—dc21   99-46912

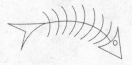

In memory of Sylvia Ashton-Warner,

and for all unorthodox teachers, especially

Margaret Lay-Dopyera of Syracuse University

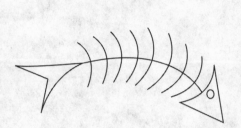

# Chapter 1

"**What** will happen now?" I asked Mamma as we watched the plane take the teacher away.

"Maybe no more school." Mamma twitched her shoulder a little to show she didn't care. Mamma never went to school much, just a few months here and there when her family wasn't trapping or out at spring muskrat camp. She said she hated school when she was little.

The little plane circled our village and then flew low over Andreson's store and waggled its wings at us. That was Sam White, the pilot, saying good-bye to us.

It was Sam White laughing, too. Sam thought nearly everything was funny. He had just landed

1

with the mail and there the new teacher was, waiting for him when he opened the door of the cockpit. She pushed right through the rest of us and started talking before Sam even got to say hello.

"Wait for me, it will only take a minute," she'd said. "Please. Take me back to town. I can't stay in this place for another second."

And he'd waited, and she'd come tumbling out of her little cabin, leaving the door open, leaving everything behind but the two suitcases she carried. It was kind of funny, how she looked. I could tell Sam thought so, the way he winked at us. And then Sam had helped her into the plane and the engine had roared and they were up and over the spruce trees and on their way.

I knew what she would tell Sam. She'd tell how Amy Barrington had got mad and had busted in her door because the teacher bought mukluks from Julia Pitka instead of her. And she'd tell about the big boys who didn't listen. And she'd tell about the fish.

When we brought our lunch to school, it

would always be fish. Salmon strips or *kk'oontseek*, dried fish eggs, to eat on pilot crackers. Or half-dried fish. The oil would get on the little kids' faces and on the desks.

"Heavens, don't you ever eat anything but fish?" And she'd make us go to the basin and try to scrub the fish smell away with lots of Fels Naptha soap, and then with a bad face she'd scrub the oily ring from the washbasin.

That one time, she pushed Plasker away from her desk when she was helping him with his arithmetic.

"You smell of *fish*," she said, real mad, with her teeth together. Plasker looked scared.

"I was helping my old man bale whitefish," he said. He was pretty nervous, wiping his hands on his pants as if that would help.

The teacher told him to sit down, and she didn't even help him with his arithmetic. There were tears in her eyes. Right there we knew she was not going to stay with us.

We had a whole bunch of teachers since they started the school here, back when I was six.

3

Some left before the year was over. Some stayed one whole school year. But none ever came back after the summer.

Sometimes we could see the look on their faces the first week they were here, cleaning out their little cabin, putting up pictures on the walls. The ones who looked mean from the very first lasted the longest. It was the ones who smiled all the time and pretended to like everything who didn't last.

Maybe they were running out of teachers and we wouldn't get another one.

But in just a week Sam brought us a new teacher.

I was helping Old Man Andreson in the store when Sam came in. It was my job to cross off every day on the calendar with an *X* so Old Man Andreson wouldn't get mixed up and forget what day it was. And it was the first day of a new month, so I had to tear that last month off, too. October 1, it was now—1948.

Sam was really big and tall, and when I was little, he always used to lift me up and make my head touch the ceiling. Now I was too big for that, so he just stuck me on top of the counter.

"Fred! I brought you a new teacher. I kidnapped her. What do you think about that?"

I had a bad feeling about that, so I asked him, "Is she nice?"

"Oh-ho," said Sam. "This one's got a little mileage. You kids are not going to get away with nothin'."

That didn't sound like she was going to be nice, so I wiggled down off the counter.

I wanted to go have a look at her.

# Chapter 2

I ran to the Nickoli house to see if Bertha was there. She was in the back of the house, helping her mother with a moose skin. They were twisting it and twisting it with a long spruce stick so it could get really soft. Good enough to sew.

"Bertha, we got a new teacher." Bertha's eyes got big and worried.

"Is she nice?"

"I don't know. Sam said she was strict."

Bertha dropped the stick and we ran, even though her mother was yelling after her to get back.

We ran to the teacher's cabin and then stopped short in the dusty road. There was a skinny woman whacking the dust out of a rug on the side of the cabin porch.

She was wearing pants. We never saw a woman wear pants. Our moms always wore dresses, with thick socks and moccasins. And us girls, too. Sometimes if it was really cold, we'd have pants under our skirts. But never just pants.

We looked hard at her to see what we could find out.

She was strong, that was for sure. The way she whacked that rug. The dust was just flying. She was making an ugly face to keep the dust out of her eyes. Then she dropped the rug in the dead grass by the door and went back inside.

We walked to her door and peeked in. She didn't even hardly look up, but she saw us.

"Good, just what I need. Two girls to give me a hand," she said. She didn't ask our names or nothing. Didn't even smile or tell us what a pretty village we had or any of the other teacher stuff. She just handed the slop bucket to Bertha and told her to dump it out back. And then she stripped the blankets off the bed and told me to hang them out back on the line.

We did what she told us for a while, and then she stopped and said, "We need some tea." Just like we were grown women.

She took the kettle off the back of the stove and poured water into a fat little brown teapot. I wanted to put my hands around that pot, it was so round.

She got three cups down from the shelf and three saucers, and took three spoons out of the jar on the table. Then she took a little silver thing and poured the tea through that so the tea leaves wouldn't get in our cups. I never saw that before.

And that tea was good. She put as much sugar in hers as we put in ours. Then she opened a can of milk and put some of that in her tea. Bertha and I looked surprised at each other. We didn't know you could put milk in tea. She saw us look and said, "Try it."

Bertha shook her head no. She never liked to do anything new. But I tried it. The tea was even better with milk than without.

The new teacher drank her tea straight down and then poured herself another cup.

"Thank heavens for tea," she said. She looked at us carefully. "Now then, who are you?" She had a funny way of talking, not like us. More short like. Like each letter made a hard sound.

"You talk funny," I said.

"That's because I'm English," she said.

I thought about that for a minute. English was what we talked. Mamma said she couldn't talk English until she was married, because then they got a radio and she learned it from the radio. So it didn't make sense, the teacher saying she was English.

The new teacher went to the shelf over her bed and took down a big book. She showed us a map. She put her finger on one part and said, "This is Alaska, where we are." And then she put her finger on the map on the other side. "This is England, where I come from." Her finger covered the place, it was so small. She looked at me and said, "The people from England are English."

"Oh," I said.

"And the language we speak is called English as well."

"Oh," I said again.

I think she could tell I was still a little mixed up, because she said, "The English that we speak in England sounds different from the way you speak English here. But it's the same language."

"Oh, yeah," I said, and this time I knew what she meant. Like how you can tell when someone is from Nulato or Hughes just because they say their words different.

"My name is Agnes Sutterfield," she said. "What are your names?"

"This is Bertha," I said. "Bertha Nickoli. She's really Bertha John, but Jake and Annie adopted her from her real mother, Sally John, because Sally had too many kids already. Sally lives at Allakaket."

The new teacher looked at Bertha. "I know your real mother," she said.

"You do?" We were very surprised.

"I taught at Allakaket a long time," she said.

"And what's your name?" she said to me.

"Fred," I said.

"Fred," said the new teacher. I could see she was waiting for something else.

"Frederika, really," I said. "There was this old man ran a store when my dad was little. Dubin, that's his name. Frederika was his mother's name. He told my dad to name me that when my dad was just a little boy. 'You name one of your daughters Frederika,' he told him. And my dad did."

"Oh," she said, and smiled. "Dubin."

"You know him, too?" asked Bertha.

"Oh, no. He was gone before my time. But I heard a lot about him." The look she had made me wish she'd tell us about Dubin, but she stood up suddenly and said, "Well, you girls have work at home, I'm sure. I'm going to finish here and start in at the school. Be sure to be there tomorrow at nine. We have a lot of catching up to do."

Bertha went back to help her mom, and I went back to the store to see if Sam was still there. If I was helping in the store, he'd always buy me a candy bar.

He'd already gone, but Old Man Andreson was talking to some of the men. Barney Sam and his big boy, George, and Clayton Malemute and them. They were buying shells for their guns, and other stuff they needed to go hunting. They never did their buying quick—they had to talk a long time. I wasn't supposed to talk when grown people were talking, but I was too curious.

"Jack," I said to Old Man Andreson. "You know our new teacher?"

"Oh, yeah," he said. "That's a good one. Agnes Sutterfield. She been in the country a long time, up at Allakaket. They like her a lot up there."

"That was my teacher," George said. "One winter we was staying with my grandma up there. I was only in that school a little while before we went to spring camp, but she was a good one. She taught me how to read. She knows a lot. That's a good teacher you got now."

# Chapter 3

This is how we came to get a school.

First everyone in the village lived at Dolbi, that's upriver. They never had a school there. It flooded so much at Dolbi that people's stuff just floated away some years. And then everyone said we better move somewhere else not so low. So the whole village moved here where we are now.

I wish I could remember that. Some of the houses at Dolbi they put on rafts and just floated them down here. I would like to have seen that.

Then Grandpa said some other people moved here because this is a good place. Lots of game.

Pretty soon the government said we had

enough kids to have a teacher if we had a place to hold school. You had to have six kids or you couldn't have a school. That was the law. So they made a school in Old Man Johnson's cabin because he was dead and no one lived in it anymore.

And that was how we got our school. And I'm glad we did, because I like school.

When I got up in the morning, I looked out the window at the schoolhouse down by the bank. It was still dark, but I could see there was already smoke coming out of the chimney.

The last teacher could never get the fire going. She had to wait for one of the big boys, Roger or Little Pete, to start it. Roger got funny one time and closed the damper when he started, so it just smoked real bad and we all had to leave the school. The teacher was so upset, she said no more school that day and she went to her cabin and shut the door. That Roger is just a nuisance.

I was so happy to be going to school again. Mamma was mad. She was slamming things around. She didn't see the use of school. It made her mad to have me gone all day when I could be helping her at home.

Bokko was helping me get ready. I couldn't find my clean socks, so she gave me hers, which were pretty clean even though there was a hole in the toe she never mended.

I put them on when Mamma wasn't looking, or she would have yelled and maybe kept me from school because I didn't have clean socks and Bokko's had a hole in them. And she'd yell at Bokko for not darning them.

I was glad to be going to school, but I felt sorry for leaving Bokko. She didn't go to school because she was deaf. She was born that way. She was two years older than me, twelve, and I was the only one who understood what she wanted to say. I could just tell somehow. Mamma wasn't patient to understand her.

It had snowed a little in the night, and I ran all the way to school with that good feeling you get when it first snows and the good feeling from going to school.

The schoolroom looked really different when I got there. The sun was just coming up and all the windows were just shining. She'd washed them, even the corners that used to be gunked up. All the kids were there before me because of those socks.

Miss Agnes had put a map on the wall, like the one she showed me and Bertha in the book. A big, big map of the whole world. It covered the whole wall, so the bottom was by my toes and the top was way over my head.

I couldn't keep my eyes off that map, it was so wonderful. Right away I went to it and I stood on a chair and I showed those kids, "This is Alaska, where we are now, and this is where Teacher comes from. It's English." The teacher looked at me with a quick look, and I could see she was pleased I remembered. On this big map my fingers didn't cover the little English place.

Miss Agnes had a record player that worked with batteries, and lots of records on the back table, and a whole bunch of big books we never saw before. She must have brought them with her. There were some pictures on the wall by the windows, some kind we never saw before. They weren't pictures of real things, but they were just lines and squares and shapes of bright, bright colors all put together, not looking like anything, but really happy somehow.

Everything was way different from any time we'd come to school before.

For another thing, the desks weren't all lined up. Miss Agnes had put them in a circle, around the edges of the room, and there was the long table in the middle of the room. And her desk was just back in the corner, not where it used to be, in front of the blackboard.

Desks in a circle looked like more fun someway. And a teacher's desk in the corner looked more friendly like, too.

Everything was different, but *good* different.

# Chapter 4

**All** the kids looked different that first day, too. Like something good was going to happen.

It was early October and the river was just slushing up, and there hadn't been hardly any snow, so all the kids were there. After freeze-up lots of them would go to winter camp to trap with their folks and would be there till Christmas.

There was me and Bertha, and the big boys, Jimmy Sam and Roger and Little Pete, and the littlest ones, Selina and Charlie-Boy, and the middle ones, Kenny and Plasker. Toby Joe, too. And Marie. She was the only big girl.

Me and Bokko were mostly the only ones who stayed in town all winter. That was because we didn't have a dad. He died when we were little. They sent him to a hospital for people who had TB. In Juneau. That's really far away. But he didn't get better.

We have a picture of him tacked on the wall at home. It was when he went to Nulato one time. There was this priest there who had a camera, and he took lots of pictures of everyone.

There's my dad leaning against the wall of the old store with a bunch of other guys. He was real young then. He has this kind of old-time hat, squashed up like. All the guys in the picture do, too. Mamma said that's the kind of hat they wore then, back in the twenties.

He has on those old kind of summer moccasins, the long kind that wrap up your leg a little ways. I know his mamma made those for him. She died before I was born, so she never knew about me and Bokko.

My dad's looking at the camera and he's laughing, with his eyes all squinched up. Bokko looks like that when she smiles, too.

I think he was a really happy kind of guy.

That's what everyone says. Always joking. If he hadn't died, there would have been more laughing in our house. Mamma is not the laughing kind.

Mamma works for Old Man Andreson at the store, cleaning and doing the washing and all of that. And she does sewing to sell, boots and mitts and marten hats. She sews really good.

She never stops working. If she isn't at the store, she's home baking bread, making duck soup, or cooking ptarmigan or whatever we have to eat that day, and when that's finished, she'll take out her sewing. Mamma thinks working hard is what everyone's supposed to do, and so she thinks school is just a waste of time.

Grandpa runs a little trapline out of the village, and he gives Mamma skins from the marten and rabbits he traps to make hats and mittens. And sometimes he gets a wolverine for ruffs, the fur trim around the hood. Wolverine is best for that because it doesn't frost up like other fur.

It's a lot of work, sewing. First she has to scrape those skins with a special little knife until they're soft and there's no fat left on them. Then she washes them and hangs them up to dry on the line by the door. Not too near the stove or they'll dry too fast. While they're drying, she keeps twisting the skins so that they won't dry stiff. Me and Bokko have to do that part, mostly.

Mamma makes mittens out of lots of different kinds of skins. Otter and wolf are good ones, and she gets a lot of money for those. The mittens have long, braided harnesses so you can tie the mittens up behind you, so they won't get in your way if you're working. And so they won't get lost.

Those harnesses are made of three different bright colors of yarn, and they're prettier than anything you ever saw. They have big pom-poms on them for decorations.

Mamma gets me and Bokko to wrap the yarn around a piece of cardboard about a million times to make those pom-poms fat enough. We get tired doing it, but in the end when Mamma cuts the ends and fluffs them out, they look so pretty.

She makes boots from caribou legs. Caribou is very warm, and the leg of the caribou is just the right shape already. When you skin the leg out, you just cut it carefully down the front and there's a fur tube, just right for boots. Mamma makes an insole of caribou fur for inside the boots, too. And at the top of the boots she sews on a beautiful band she makes with beads. She always makes flowers on her bands.

Grandma says in the old days they made the design on the bands with porcupine quills. You have to flatten the porcupine quill with your fingernail, and then you sew it flat to the band. Oh, first you dye the quills different colors. I'd like to see that kind of band, but no one makes it anymore. Too much work, I guess. They use beads instead.

There's a lot of stuff they don't make anymore that my grandma tells me about, like the rabbit-skin underwear she had when she was little. Long ago you only wore what the women could make, but now people have got catalogs and the store.

Mamma doesn't make our parkas. She always orders them from the Sears, Roebuck catalog because she thinks making parkas is too much trouble.

Grandma doesn't like that ordering stuff. She grumbles at Mamma in Indian and calls her lazy. Grandma would make parkas for us herself, but she doesn't sew very much anymore because her eyes are going bad. It doesn't *seem* like her eyes are bad, because she sees everything me and Bokko and Mamma do, but that's what she says.

Grandma makes the sinew thread for sewing out of that big hump on the back of the moose, and she tans the moose hide with rotten moose brains. Boy, does *that* smell bad.

She's the one who taught me and Bokko to knit and to sew. Mamma doesn't have patience for it. She always yells at us when we do something wrong, and then Grandma will frown at her and say, *"Sikoya,"* in this way she has, and put her arms out to us. That means "grandchild."

Grandma and Grandpa are too old to go out to camp much, so they stay in town all winter, too. They didn't have any sons, only Mamma, so it's bad for them that way. There's too much hard work at the trapline for just women and one old man.

There's marten trapping in the winter, and after Christmas people go back out to their winter trapping camps for beaver.

Spring camp, when people hunt muskrats, is just before the snow melts, and then we have fish camp in the summer. We all go to fish camp, me and Bokko and Mamma and sometimes Grandma and Grandpa, too. That's because all our cousins and aunts and uncles go there, too, so there's not so much work. We can all take turns, like.

Grandpa misses going out trapping, but he says he gets more money making snowshoes than he would trapping anyway. Old Man Andreson buys those to sell in Fairbanks and other places, and he says he could sell as many as Grandpa could turn out, because Grandpa's snowshoes are made of birch, so they're real light on your feet.

First Grandpa has to get just the right kind of birch. It has to be straight, with no knots. Then he soaks that birch in water until it's soft, just right to tie onto the snowshoe frames.

After they're ready to come off the frames, Grandma fills in the insides of the snowshoes with those rawhide strips she makes from moose hide. It's really hard to fill those snowshoes, all crisscrossed like a spider web. I want to learn how.

There were lots of things we could learn at home, but I liked the stuff we learned at school, too, and I wanted to get good at reading so I could read fast like Old Man Andreson. When the paper comes in the mail from Fairbanks, he reads out loud in the store to everyone, and he goes so fast everyone tells him to slow down. I'd like to read that fast.

So mostly I was glad we got to stay in town all winter.

# Chapter 5

**After** we'd looked at all the books and stuff, Miss Agnes told us all to sit down. Little Pete and Roger pretended like they were going to sit in the same chair by Marie, and they pushed each other and wrestled.

I waited for the teacher to holler at them and hit her desk with the ruler, but she just looked a look at them, with her eyebrow up and her mouth a little pushed to one side. It wasn't a mean look, it was a smart look, if you know what I mean. So they stopped and sat down.

It was no fun trying to get this teacher upset because it didn't look like she could be upset.

Miss Agnes was different some way.

She told us to take all our old books out and put them on the desk. There were geography books and history books, and reading books and penmanship books you made little circles in. They were pretty beat-up. They weren't even new when we first got our school, just hand-me-downs from other schools that didn't need them.

She had us put all those books away in cardboard boxes, and she told Little Pete and Roger that after school they'd have to put them in the cache where we stored everything we didn't need. She even put the ugly old grade book in the boxes. "I don't believe in grades," she said. Boy, that was good news.

We sure never started school throwing books out before. We didn't know what to think.

Then the teacher put a big box on the long table, and we gathered around to watch while she unwrapped it. When she opened the box, it smelled so good, like new pencils. And that was because there were pencils in it. Not just the yellow kind we always had, but boxes and boxes of colored pencils, with every color of lead you could think of.

And there were big yellow boxes of crayons, forty-eight in a box, the skinny kind, not the fat kind we had before. And a box of green pencils with dark lead, and lots and lots of tin boxes of paints. Each one had a little brush in it, and there was another bunch of little brushes tied together with a rubber band.

And there was a wooden box with little metal tubes that Miss Agnes said had paint in them, too. I couldn't believe she was going to let us use all those beautiful things.

But Miss Agnes started to lay the things out on the long table. And then she brought out paper from another box. Medium-sized paper, and some big paper, bigger than we ever saw before. "The first thing you must do," she said, "is to brighten this school up. Everyone will make a picture for the wall."

Miss Agnes showed us how to rule a margin for our picture so there would be a white space all around. That was for a frame. She told us we could use the big paper or the little paper, and we could make a picture of anything we liked but we had to fill in all the white space inside the frame with color. Miss Agnes said that was the difference between a fine painting and a drawing.

She showed us how to wipe our brushes carefully while we were painting. And then she helped the littlest ones, Selina and Charlie-Boy.

They took the big boxes of crayons and made a dark line with every single crayon. They held the crayon so hard their fingers turned white. They wanted to know the names of every color. They had funny names, not like the plain names on our old fat crayons.

We laughed and laughed when Miss Agnes said the names. Burnt sienna and magenta and periwinkle. Flesh. That was very funny.

We all put that flesh crayon by our hands and laughed because our skin and that crayon weren't anything like the same color. Even when we put it by Miss Agnes's hand it wasn't the same color. We didn't know who would have skin that color.

Miss Agnes sort of snorted and said, "No one."

Pretty soon everyone got just quiet, we were so happy making our pictures.

Miss Agnes put a record on the record player. It was singing, only the voices were really high and sliding around like. Once I heard that same kind of music in Koyukuk. Dominic Carlotti, who owned the store there, played it on his record player, only Dominic's was scratchier than Miss Agnes's record, so it seemed old. This seemed new and bright. In some different language. The sunshine was filling the room from those bright windows, and that music was going up, up, in some kind of way. I felt excited inside, like when the stern-wheeler is coming up the river for the first time after the ice breaks up.

"Dominic has that kind of music," I told her.

"Yes, he does," she said. "Dominic likes opera. It's the favorite kind of music where he comes from. He's Italian," she said. I looked at the big map. She walked to it and said, "Here. This one that looks like a boot. That's where Dominic comes from."

I had never thought of people coming from anywhere before, and now I knew two new places. English and the boot.

When all those pictures were on the wall, we couldn't stop looking at them. Everyplace we looked was some bright color.

Little Pete made a picture of his dad's trapline cabin out by Nicholi Slough. It was so good, with a blue sky and these good little snowshoes he drew with a pen the teacher gave him that you dip in black ink. He was proud of that picture, I could tell, because he kept making fun of it.

And Selina made one of her baby sister in the new boots her mom made for her. That picture was funny because the baby was real small but the boots took up nearly the whole page.

Roger made a good picture of Sam White's airplane, and he asked Miss Agnes how to spell *Gullwing Stinson* so he could write that at the bottom. Roger really liked airplanes, and he knew all the different names they had and all about their engines and stuff.

Kenny did the stern-wheeler, George Black's *Idler*, that comes up the Koyukuk River every year with all our freight. It's hard to draw it right, because there are a hundred paddles on the wheel that pushes the boat, but Kenny did it good.

I wanted to make a picture of the music she was playing, but I didn't know how, so I made a picture of Miss Agnes. It was hard to get her hair, some gray and some not gray, all flying around her head somehow, not pulled neat like Mamma's or the other women.

When it was time for lunch, I felt a little worried. The other kids did, too, I could tell. Plasker most of all.

Miss Agnes had made some tea from the pot on the stove, and she told us if we all brought cups from home tomorrow, we could have some, too.

She must have made a batch of bread after Bertha and I left her the day before, because she had a sandwich to eat with her tea. Peanut butter.

We got really quiet while we were eating, and

all the kids had their heads down, looking at their desks. Miss Agnes looked at us a little strangely.

Finally I asked her. "Do you like fish, Miss Agnes?" It was very quiet. All the kids looked at her from under their eyebrows to see what she'd say.

"No." She made a face. "I hate fish." That was bad. I tried to cover my fish strips with my hand. Miss Agnes looked at all of us with a question on her face.

"Our old teacher didn't like the smell of fish," I said.

"Oh," Miss Agnes said. "Well, *I* can't smell anything. I have sinus trouble." We all looked at each other.

So that was good.

# Chapter 6

**After** lunch that first day Miss Agnes said she needed to find out how much writing we had learned. I was not happy to do this, because I hadn't learned much.

She gave us new pencils, and paper with lines, and told us all to write our names and the day we were born. The older ones were to write something about themselves, just anything to show Miss Agnes what we could do.

We all looked at Bertha because Bertha was so good at writing. Seemed like she was writing all the time.

Even before we went to school, she used to get a pencil from Old Man Andreson and she'd hunker down by the boxes in the store and she'd copy the writing. She'd write *Olympia Beer* and *Pillsbury Flour* and anything that was printed on the boxes. She didn't know what the letters said, she just thought they were pretty.

Old Man Andreson wrote the alphabet the way it goes on a piece of paper for her.

"Bertha, you'll be my secretary when you grow up," he told her.

She never let loose of that piece of paper. It was always in her pocket. She'd copy the letters in the snow with a stick, or in the mud on the riverbank. Bertha was funny that way.

Miss Agnes stopped in surprise when she saw Bertha's writing.

"Well, Bertha." She bent to look carefully at each letter. "It would be hard to improve on that," she said. Bertha looked really shining like, having Miss Agnes see what a good writer she was.

"I'll teach you how to write cursive now. You're ready."

I knew what that was, that curly kind of writing

some grown-ups used, just flying across the paper, ninety miles an hour. I couldn't wait to learn that, too.

Marie looked like she was going to cry. She was fourteen, but she'd only spent a few months in school off and on. Her mom had all those babies Marie had to take care of when her mom went to help her dad on the trapline. She couldn't write much at all. She put her head down.

Miss Agnes walked around and looked at everyone's writing. Charlie-Boy and Selina could write their names, but that was all.

None of us were very good at writing, except Bertha.

Miss Agnes took a roll of masking tape from her shelf and put a strip on each desk. She wrote the alphabet in printing on that strip with a pen. She wrote the big letters and then the little letters. Then she taped a paper on our desk with our name written in perfect letters. That was to help us remember. For Bertha she wrote the letters in cursive.

Then she started to show the rest of us on the

blackboard what each letter was supposed to look like, starting with the vowels, because she said you used one of those in every word, so the vowels had to be really good. Like if on a shopping list you wrote an *o* so it looked like an *e*, you might get a pet instead of a pot. She made it funny, showing us how awful letters looked when they were made silly.

Miss Agnes called a sloppy *o* a "hairy *o*" because when you don't write an *o* right, it looks like a little face with one hair sticking up on top. We really laughed at that. And she said the nose of an *e* was supposed to be sharp enough to prick your finger on. Then she drew a finger getting pricked by that sharp point on the *e*.

We never tried to do it right before, we just wrote any which way. So we were surprised to find Miss Agnes was going to be so picky. She said if we wrote our letters sloppy, she would give us back our work and make us do it over.

You'd think it would make me mad to do that, but it made me glad. Like when my grandma makes me do something over and over till I get it right. I feel like she's going to make sure I learn it good, and so I don't feel mad. That's how I felt now.

We practiced on our paper, making sharp-nosed *e*'s and perfect *o*'s that weren't hairy, and straight *i*'s with the dot right smack on top, not drifting away somewhere. Charlie-Boy made us laugh, because he was practicing so hard his tongue was sticking out.

It was fun the way we did it, and I wanted to make every letter just perfect. I could write as perfect as Miss Agnes and Bertha if I just practiced.

While we practiced our printing, Miss Agnes read to us for half an hour, walking up and down in front of the windows while the snowflakes came tumbling down, that kind that's real big and slow falling.

It was a story called *Robin Hood,* about a man who stole money from the rich people and gave the money to the poor people who needed it. It was an olden-time story from when people had bows and arrows.

When Miss Agnes read to us, she did all the people in different voices, and we forgot right away it was just reading. It got real, like being inside the book.

I didn't want Miss Agnes to ever stop reading. I felt as if I really was in that dark, deep forest with trees taller than you ever heard of, and when she stopped, I felt shocked, as if I'd come out of a dream.

The boys were all excited to think of people fighting with big, fat sticks like that, like when Robin Hood and Little John were on the bridge. We don't have any big sticks around here, just spruce poles.

And we all thought it was funny because the book had a Little John and we had a Little Pete. And they were both really big, not little.

When she put the book back on her desk, Miss Agnes took one of the big pieces of paper and made a picture of Robin Hood. She could draw really good, and fast, too. Zip, zip, zip, and there was a man.

We all laughed when she made him have long

underwear, with funny moccasins that had pointed toes, and a short shirt, and a hat like Gilbert Dendoff was wearing when he came home from the army, except Robin Hood's hat had a feather in it.

Then she took a box of colored chalk and colored him in. Green clothes because that was like the Merry Men's uniform. And that was Robin Hood.

Marie wanted a picture of Maid Marian. Marie was all worried that Robin wouldn't see his girlfriend again because he was an outlaw, but Miss Agnes wouldn't tell us any of the story ahead of time. Not even a hint.

# Chapter 7

**Miss** Agnes used the big map to teach us geography. She pointed out the continents with a yardstick, and then she showed us how to find Alaska every time.

We had to look for the old man's beard and the fat nose. The beard was all islands. The Aleutian Islands. I never knew about those.

Then she took out a folded-up map, a map of just Alaska. It was as big as two desks, so we pushed Little Pete's and Roger's desks together, and there we were.

There was the Koyukuk River, our river, and the Yukon, down below us, and all the villages, even Dolbi, our old village that no one lived in

41

anymore. And there was Fairbanks and Anchorage. All the little creeks were there, and the long lakes and the sloughs.

Little Pete and Roger got just excited, showing us where their trapline was, and where they set the blackfish trap, and where their dad shot the bear.

It was so interesting, somehow, seeing it there on paper. I never saw the big boys so excited about anything in school.

I asked Miss Agnes where Juneau was, and she showed me, way down at the bottom, in the part she said was called the panhandle because that part looked liked a long handle and the rest of Alaska like the pan. I ran my finger from where we were on the Koyukuk River to Juneau and thought of Daddy making that long trip. It was a long way away to go to die.

Miss Agnes said she was going to teach us every one of the countries on the big map, so we'd know everything about the world. There were places where it was hot all the time and where they had never seen snow. There were places where it was cold in the winter and hot in the summer.

I could hardly wait.

After Miss Agnes folded up the big Alaska map, she gave us all a paper with arithmetic on it. She'd made one for each of us, but they were all different. Charlie-Boy's and Selina's just had numbers on them, and places to draw things. To see if they could count, like.

I was ten, so my paper had some hard adding and some take-aways. Marie's and Little Pete's and Roger's had lots more on it than mine did.

I always hated this arithmetic, and I always just wrote any old numbers down before, so I wouldn't have to think about it. And if the teachers wanted to make me do it right, I would cry and carry on. Then they would leave me alone about it.

Even if writing was fun when Miss Agnes showed us how, there was no way she could make this arithmetic fun.

After she walked around to see how many of us could do the figuring on our papers, she told us the story of Sam Dubin. That's the old man who had the mother named Frederika. Sam Dubin came from far away, too, a place above the boot. Yugoslovakia or something. And then he made a store here long ago, up around Allakaket.

He made a lot of money because there were a lot of mining camps around here in the old days. And those miners would buy anything. But that old Dubin couldn't read, and he couldn't do arithmetic, only a little. After a while people began to cheat him.

And he lost all his money. He had to go back to where he came from, broke. All that money he got cheated out of because he couldn't do this arithmetic.

Miss Agnes was going to teach us so no one could cheat us. Like if we went to a trader in Fairbanks and sold our furs, when they added it up, we'd know if they shorted us. Or if we went to a store and gave them money, we'd know if they gave us back the wrong change. Or charged us too much. It could happen if you're not smart.

So right there I made up my mind I was going to get good at this number stuff.

After school Little Pete ran home and got his dad, Big Pete, to come and look at the map of Alaska. I was staying after to help Miss Agnes. I didn't want to go home. I didn't want school to end, even.

Big Pete was embarrassed to come into the school, I could tell. He didn't speak English too good, so he just nodded his head up and down when Miss Agnes talked to him.

But he got all excited over the map, too, and started to talk in Athabascan to Little Pete. One place on the map he said was wrong. Some way the creek turned, like. Seemed like they looked at that map a long time, and then they finally left.

It was really funny about Big Pete, because he was the littlest man you ever saw. He was just a little bigger than me. Mamma said he was always like that, just a little thing. And then he got married to Lena and they had Little Pete, and that's when they started to call him Big Pete, but now

Little Pete was way bigger than his father, way bigger than anyone else in the village. Little Pete was just a giant, and he was still growing, Grandpa said. His head just scraped the top of the school door. And Big Pete was like a wolverine, Grandpa said. He could get madder than anyone, and if he was mad at Little Pete, it would look so funny, him yelling up at Little Pete, and Little Pete just looking down at him, scared like. Little Pete was as gentle and kind as a big moose and here he had this scrappy little father.

After they left, I helped Miss Agnes wipe the desks off with hot, soapy water. And then Miss Agnes washed the blackboard so it was perfect again. I couldn't do it like that. I always got it smeary. I watched her long, skinny arms, up and down, up and down. She moved so fast always.

"Miss Agnes," I said, "why did you quit teaching school at Allakaket?"

"Goodness, it was about time I quit. All those children must have got tired of me long ago." She looked at me to see if that was enough answer, but she could see it wasn't, so she got serious.

"It was time for me to go home," she said. "I haven't been to England for a very long time. I didn't mean to stay in this country so long. It was only to be a few years. Then the war started, and I didn't want to go back to England when the war was on."

I knew about that war. Gilbert Dendoff had gone to fight in that war, and Old Man Andreson was always listening to the radio and reading the newspapers and talking to the old men about it. He used to get pretty excited.

I had forgotten about that war. I was really little when it ended.

"My mother wrote me every year to come home."

I looked at her with interest. To think of Miss Agnes having a mother. What could her mother be like?

"Does she wear pants?" I asked.

Miss Agnes laughed. "Goodness, no. And she'd have had a fit if she'd ever seen me in them."

"Well, then, how come you didn't go to England after you left Allakaket? Did Sam really kidnap you?"

She put one eyebrow up in a funny way she had. "I was almost on my way when he came by the hotel in Fairbanks with Dr. Ryan. The superintendent. Dr. Ryan said he had a hard time getting this school set up, and he was going to lose it if I didn't take the job. Just for one year, until he could find someone else."

"Oh," I said again. "I'm glad Sam did that." Then I thought of how long it had been since she'd been home. "Was your mother sad that you're not coming?"

Miss Agnes gathered all the pencils on her desk together and put them in her drawer. "My mother died two years ago," she said.

"Miss Agnes will only stay here a year," I told Bertha. Bertha looked sad.

"I knew it," she said. "I hope I learn to spell real good before she goes. Then I can write her letters."

# Chapter 8

The next day I forgot my lunch and Bokko brought it to me. She knocked on the door and then stepped in, looking frightened. She put the lunch on my desk and started out the door.

Miss Agnes looked very surprised. She put her hand on Bokko's shoulder. Bokko looked at the floor.

"Where did you come from?" she asked Bokko. When Bokko didn't answer, Miss Agnes looked at me.

"She's deaf," I said. "She can't hear you, and she can't talk."

"Deaf," said Miss Agnes, still surprised. "Why hasn't she been coming to school?"

The others looked at Miss Agnes as if she were crazy. "She can't learn nothing, she's *deaf*," said Charlie-Boy.

"Nonsense," said Miss Agnes. "Why hasn't she been sent out to a school for the deaf? Is she related to you?" she asked me.

"She's my sister," I said.

"How old is she?"

"She's twelve, like me," said Toby Joe.

"Do you both live with your mother?"

"Yes," I said.

"Does your mother know about schools for the deaf?"

"Yes," I said. "Grandpa made her bring Bokko to this school the first year the school opened. That teacher said she didn't know how to teach deaf kids and Bokko had to go to a special school. Mamma got mad. She said Bokko don't need no school. She said it's bum to go so far away. Bokko's learning to cook. And she can sew pretty good."

Everyone was feeling pretty nervous now because Miss Agnes was not happy about Bokko.

"She must come to school from now on," said Miss Agnes. "I'll speak to your mother."

She took Bokko by the hand. "The rest of you finish your lunch. I'm going to have a little talk with Bokko." She put her arm around Bokko and pointed to her. "You," she said. Bokko understood that. Then Miss Agnes looked at me. "Bokko. What kind of a name is that?"

"I don't know. That's just what Grandma started to call her when she was little. Some kind of Indian name, I think."

"Well, does she have another name?"

"I don't think so," I said.

"How do you spell it?"

"I don't know. I never saw anyone spell it."

"Well, I never," said Miss Agnes. We never saw her surprised yet, but Bokko sure did it.

She started to write Bokko's name on a piece of paper. "You," she said. She pointed to Bokko and then to her name written on the paper. Then she put the pencil in Bokko's hand and held her hand so that Bokko wrote her name, too. "You are Bokko." She did it again and again so that Bokko would know.

And then she took a piece of that tape and wrote Bokko's name on the empty desk. Bokko pinched her lips together and looked at all of us. We looked at each other.

Miss Agnes was going to teach Bokko.

I don't know what Miss Agnes said to Mamma, but Bokko did come to school. Not the very next day, because Mamma was kicking up a big fuss about Bokko having no clothes and her socks having holes in them, but the day after.

Mamma had a big fight with Grandpa about it. She said who was going to help her at home if me and Bokko were in school, and what good would school do Bokko if she couldn't hear anything anyway, and she wished there was never a school here, and that skinny white woman was too nosy.

But Grandpa told Mamma to *dalek*, be quiet, and he told her he always knew there was a way for

Bokko to learn, and that the skinny white woman was a good woman who would help our Bokko.

When Mamma stamped out the door, Grandpa lit his old pipe, and then he pointed it at me and said real crabby, "Your mamma had a hard life, you know. It's hard to have a baby born deaf, and then your daddy got sick and went away and died. A hard-luck person like that could get kind of mean. You got to think about that."

Like I was the one who yelled at her, and not him.

When Sam White flew in with the mail that afternoon, Miss Agnes had a long talk with him at the store, and the next time Sam came in with the mail, there were special books for Bokko. Sign language. A way Bokko could learn to talk with her hands.

This sign language is really something. Miss Agnes said when people have been doing it a long time, their hands just fly. I'd like to see that.

And that's not all deaf people can learn to

do. Miss Agnes said there's a way deaf people can learn to look at your mouth when you're talking and know what you're saying that way. She said they would teach that to Bokko in a special school for the deaf if she went.

We all got tickled with that idea and started talking to each other without making a sound. Only we made our mouths really stick out when we did it. It was so funny, Charlie-Boy fell off his chair laughing. Then Roger started saying bad words in Indian with his mouth, and everyone started giggling.

Then Miss Agnes told us about a way that blind people can read. We were pretty interested in that because of old Blind Simon. He's been blind for a long time, because he got whipped across the eyes with a willow branch when he was out trapping, that's what he told us. I bet he would like to know about this blind reading.

We all practiced making bumps on our paper by pushing a pin through and then trying to see if we could tell how many bumps there were when we had our eyes closed. That was really hard.

Roger had scars all over his hands and fingers from that time he burned himself putting gas in the stove to start a fire. So Roger said he couldn't feel a single bump with his fingers.

Miss Agnes said he'd better take very good care of his eyes, then. Roger looked pretty serious about that.

Here we used to think some things were so bad you just had to give in to them, like being deaf or blind, but now we were finding out that there's always something they've thought of to help people like that. It was hard to do, this sign language and blind reading, but it's better to kick some instead of just sinking.

While we were doing our morning work, the writing and the arithmetic, Miss Agnes would work with Bokko.

Together they learned the alphabet. You do this alphabet with just one hand, because if you use two hands, then deaf people can't talk if they're holding something.

Miss Agnes would show Bokko the picture of

the letter in the book, and then Bokko would make the sign, and then Miss Agnes would have her write the letter on paper, the little letter and the big one. And Miss Agnes'd say the letter, and Bokko would make her mouth go the way Miss Agnes's did.

We all learned the sign language alphabet. We couldn't help but watch them. Bokko learned it faster than Miss Agnes. And Charlie-Boy learned it faster than anybody.

"Goodness," Miss Agnes would say in a disgusted way. "I wish I had a six-year-old brain."

Charlie-Boy could do all kinds of things like that, really. He was only six, but when we played ball games, he would be the best thrower and the best catcher.

He could run faster than anyone and he could climb up to the top of the tree like a squirrel, and do all these somersaults and cartwheels.

He wasn't any good at school stuff, really. He wasn't really good at anything you sat still for. But he was the best at sign language.

Miss Agnes watched him and said, "I think

sign language is as much an athletic skill as a language." She meant if you're good at stuff like Charlie-Boy, you'd do the sign language easier.

Soon Bokko could ask all of us to tell her our name, and we would do it in sign language, and then we'd ask her her name, and she'd sign it for us.

Bokko was so happy, knowing everyone's real name. Bokko had made up names for all of us in the village, but only I knew what they meant. Like Old Man Andreson, he had such a big belly that Bokko would curve her hand above her stomach for his name. And for Mamma, she'd pretend to make a bow of the apron strings Mamma always tied around her front, and I knew who that meant.

And then Miss Agnes said it was too long to spell out everyone's name in signs, so we just used initials. I was Fred, so she told Bokko to make the little *F* sign over her heart to show I was her sister.

After Mamma wasn't acting so crabby about Bokko coming to school, Bokko went home one day and tapped Mamma on the arm to make her pay attention. Then she made the sign for *Mamma,* her thumb under her chin.

"That means 'Mamma,'" I said.

Then Bokko smiled that smile she got from our daddy, and she made the sign for *pretty.*

"That means you are pretty, Mamma," I said.

Mamma's face went so stiff for a minute that I felt nervous. And then she ducked her head away and went on with her sewing.

"You girls act foolish," she said in a sort of funny voice, not looking at us.

The next day Mamma wrapped up a loaf of her good bread in a towel and told us to take it to school for Miss Agnes. We were so surprised, we just stared at her for a minute.

Mamma frowned at us as mean as she could.

"That teacher don't look like she eats *nothing,*" she said. Like it was our fault Miss Agnes was so skinny.

That's how we knew Mamma wasn't mad at Miss Agnes anymore.

# Chapter 9

In November Little Pete had to go to the trapline with his grandpa and his dad and his uncles. Little Pete's auntie Bernie usually went to winter camp with them and did all the cooking.

Little Pete's mom was dead, that's why. A long time ago, when Little Pete was just born, they had measles at our old village of Dolbi. Those measles killed a lot of people, mostly the old people and the babies, but Little Pete's mom died then.

Big Bernie, we always called his aunt. She was really big, like Little Pete, and could do anything a man could do. Once she even made a cabin by herself. Eight logs high, Grandpa said, and it was a good one, too.

Usually Little Pete was dying to get out to camp as soon as it snowed. He really liked it out there at their camp because he liked being out in the woods. But he didn't really want to go this year because school was so interesting with Miss Agnes there. Most of all he didn't want to miss the end of *Robin Hood*. He wasn't good enough at reading to read it for himself, so Miss Agnes read extra long the last day he was in school, and we finished the book.

So Little Pete was glad of that. And Miss Agnes gave him a little notebook and told him to write in it every day so he wouldn't forget all he'd learned about printing nicely.

A few weeks later Roger went to camp, too. Roger's family was very big. There were nine kids altogether, and he was the only one still going to school. The oldest ones hadn't gone very much. And there were the little ones who didn't go to school yet. The twins were four, and Frankie was two years old, and there was a new one, the baby, Liza.

There was a lot of hoorah in the village when Roger's family got ready to go, because they were taking three dog teams. We all stood out in the street at recess time and watched them leave.

All the dogs in town were barking and pulling at their chains, wishing they could go, too.

Roger's oldest brother was loading up the freight sled Roger was going to drive, and those dogs were just jerking in their harnesses and barking, wanting to get out on the trail. Roger was standing on the brake with both feet, and he could just barely keep the dogs from moving the sled. It was funny to watch.

The sleds were piled high with bales of dried dogfish and food and all the stuff they needed at camp. They didn't tie it down real careful the way most people did. It was just kind of thrown in there. They were a happy family, happy-go-lucky.

Nearly every day some other family would go

off to winter camp and the village was getting emptier and emptier.

Soon Marie Solomon had to stay home from school to take care of the kids because her mom was going out to help her dad trap. Miss Agnes told Marie to come to her cabin at night and they could keep up their reading together.

Marie was always having to stay with those kids. Her mom had one nearly every year, and there was another one coming. I knew there were two still in diapers, because I helped Marie hang out the washing when I had time. I liked to help Marie because she was always so happy.

She had to do the wash every day in the old gas washer just to keep up with the diapers. That took a lot of water.

We had to melt snow to get water in the winter. Sometimes Grandpa and the other men would cut big chunks of ice from the lake behind the village, too. Ice makes lots more water than snow. In the summer we all got water from the river.

And Marie had to cook all the meals for those

kids when her folks were gone, and make bread. It was a lot of work.

Still, she had time to curl her hair in these rods she had from the Sears catalog, and she made it look like in the magazines, turned back away from her face. And she kept that house clean, too. The floor was always swept. My grandma thought she was a really good girl. She was just proud of her.

But Mamma didn't think much of Marie because she was always singing to the radio when you came in that house. Mamma thought work was too serious for singing. And because Marie was always the one who danced most and the longest when we had a dance. All of Roger's big brothers and whoever was there from some other villages, they all wanted to dance with Marie. That made Mamma look sour when that happened.

Miss Agnes didn't like Marie having to take care of all those kids herself, I could tell. "You need to know how to read and write to get along in life," Miss Agnes said to Marie. But I could tell Marie thought she already knew how to do everything she needed to know to get along in life. She was proud she could already do everything a woman was supposed to do.

I think Miss Agnes worried about Marie because she didn't learn fast. Or maybe because Marie was so good-natured, she'd do what anybody said. Anyway, she kept Marie at it, even if she wasn't coming to school with us.

Marie wasn't the only one. Plasker's father came to Miss Agnes's cabin sometimes at night, and she helped him learn to read and write, and even Old Man Toby came to learn to write his name.

Miss Agnes didn't think school was just for kids.

"You have to keep learning all your life," she said.

That was a good thing to think about, always learning something new. It wasn't like you had to hurry up and learn everything right away before the learning time was over, it was like you could kind of relax and take your time and enjoy it.

# Chapter 10

There were a lot of different things we did in school with Miss Agnes that were fun. More fun than we ever had in school before.

She had a little squeeze box like some of the old miners had. A concertina hers was called. Theirs were bigger and square, and hers was little and sort of round with straight edges. She told us, but I forget what you call that shape.

Sometimes, any old time of the day, we never could tell when, she'd take it out of its little case and we'd sing. She taught us "Polly Wolly Doodle" and "Barb'ry Allen" and "Loch Lomond" and a million other songs.

We'd ask her for the new songs we heard on

the radio, and we'd sing them for her, and she'd play those, too. She was really good at "Hey, Good Lookin" and stuff like that. She'd put Bokko's hand on the squeeze box while she played, and Bokko could feel the music, like.

Sometimes at night on the weekends we have music and dancing in the community hall. Different times, like somebody's birthday or when everyone came in from beaver trapping. Or a potlatch, that we have for someone who's died. There are two or three nights of dances with a potlatch.

Martin Olin always plays for dances. He has this violin he ordered from Sears, a really good one, and he could play like anything. Hog River Dan has a steel guitar and Bobby Kennedy has a mandolin, and they sound really good together.

Martin has this one song, "Cindy," that he always plays on the violin, and it's so happy that no one can sit still and everyone'll dance, and they'll dance so hard that the dust comes up from the floorboards in puffs, like it's keeping time with the music.

Even all us kids dance, and Charlie-Boy is the best of all. All the old ladies like to dance with Charlie-Boy because he's so lively. Bokko can dance just like anyone because she feels the music in her feet someway. Mamma dances, too, and sometimes she even smiles and laughs a little. Then she looks young almost.

Almost everyone has a best song that they sing if the dance goes on long enough. Martha always sings "I'm So Lonesome I Could Cry," and she makes her voice just whiny like Hank Williams on the record. And so sad. It's really good, the way she sings that.

This is how it is at a dance. The men line up on one side of the wall and the women on the other, and when a man wants to dance, he comes over and just kicks a woman on the leg, just a little bit, to show he wants to dance with her. And then they dance, and then there's a circle, when everyone walks around with his partner around the room, and then they play another song and you dance again. That way you dance twice with the same person.

Grandma says that's the way they learned it from the old miners who came into the country when she was a girl. That's how everyone learned to play the guitar and stuff, from those old-timers and from listening to the radio.

When we had a dance, we'd go get Miss Agnes and she'd bring her squeeze box, and that way she could play and the guys who were doing the music could have a turn to dance. Boy, she knew some good ones, too, ones she never played us in school because they didn't have words to sing. They were just like Martin's songs, you couldn't sit still.

But Miss Agnes would never dance. She'd just watch us and laugh.

# Chapter 11

**One** day Miss Agnes made a long line on the wall with skinny white paper from Andreson's adding machine. And then she put numbers on that line to show how the years went. The numbers went backward till they got to the zero, and then they went forward. The picture of Robin Hood was at the 1100 number, and then whenever we had history, we'd put another picture up.

Nineteen forty-eight, that was us today, and 1938 was a war picture. Miss Agnes made a picture of bombs dropping on England for that. And down at the other end she made a picture of cavemen, the long-ago people. And a picture of Russians coming to Alaska in the 1700 place.

It was good to have that line. We could see how long ago things were happening with it. It made my thinking go straight.

When that line was almost filled up, we played time machine. We pretended we had a time machine like that guy in this book Miss Agnes told us about, and we'd pick a time to go back to, and we'd pretend to land in a long-ago time, and then we'd tell everyone what we saw when we were there, back in time.

That was really fun. Kenny made us laugh and laugh when he talked old-timey like Robin Hood and them. "Methinks I see a damsel!" and stuff like that.

But you had to know what we'd learned to play time machine, because everyone would ask questions and try to trip you up. Miss Agnes never gave us tests, she just had us do things like this that made us remember what we learned. So it was really harder than a test, but it didn't seem like it somehow.

Sometimes in the middle of anything she'd turn to one of us and say, "Name the continents," or "What do you call animals without back-bones?" Any kind of question she'd ask us from what we'd studied before.

It made everything stick in our minds better when we knew she was going to do that any old time. Even the little ones could remember really hard things that way.

After school sometimes I'd go over to Grandpa's and I'd tell him about the stuff we learned in history and science. He really liked me to do that.

I asked Miss Agnes if I could have some of that skinny paper, and I made Grandpa one of those time lines, too. I couldn't make the pictures on it good, like my teacher, but after I told Grandpa, he knew what they were supposed to be.

Grandpa never knew anything about the Romans and people like that. When I made that skirt thing they wear in my picture, he laughed and laughed.

He couldn't read hardly any, but he liked to look at that thing a lot.

Grandma kicked up a fuss, though, and said

she didn't want that paper thing on her wall, and so Grandpa rolled it up and would look at it when she wasn't there. He would show his friends when they came to visit, and they liked it just as much as he did.

Grandpa put the year he was born, 1878, on the line, and his friend old George put the year we moved from Dolbi. The picture about World War I was the one they talked about the most because I'd written under it what Miss Agnes had put on our time line: ten million dead, twenty-one million wounded.

They couldn't get over that. Here they were trapping and hunting and raising their families, and away on the other side of the world this thing was happening, and they hardly knew, because there weren't radios then.

Grandpa doesn't like to stay in the village so much. He likes to be out in the woods all the time, but he's too old to go by himself. So he and the other old men sit around together and drink tea and talk about the old times. We like to sit and listen to that, us kids.

Grandpa remembers when there were lots and lots of white men in the country. The ones who came to Wiseman and those places to get gold. The Indians helped lots of them when they got in trouble, like when they were out on the trail and they nearly froze.

And sometimes those white men helped the Indians, too. Like when someone got sick, one of those men had the medicine for it. They got along good together, Grandpa says.

A lot of people around here have grandpas who were those old miners.

But Grandpa still works hard. He sets a net under the river ice in the winter, and he helps Plasker's mom with her fish trap. People give him moose and caribou, but he snares rabbits and ptarmigan to eat. And he and Grandma go to fish camp with us in the summer.

What he misses is when he and his father would go way up north to hunt mountain sheep. Or caribou and moose. Those were his best times, he says. There weren't any moose or caribou around our village in the old days. They hardly saw them. So they had to travel a long way to get them.

He tells us the stories his mamma told him, about before there were any white men in the country. His mamma and them used to make a sod house, half underground, and they'd live in there in the winter and be just warm.

And they traveled all the time to find meat to eat. No villages then. When they started a school in Allakaket, his mamma told him to go to school. She wanted him to learn to read and talk English. She was smart that way, he says. She knew he would need to know that stuff, the way things were changing. And she thought maybe if he went to school, he'd have an easier life than she'd had.

He went the first time when he was twelve. He says they didn't use paper then, only slates to write on with chalk.

He went there for a couple of years, just in the fall before winter camp, so he only got through just the first-grade work.

That's why he liked to hear about all the stuff he missed in the other grades.

One of the best things of all was when Miss Agnes ordered a little microscope for us, and we could look down inside it and see things that lived in the water. That was a thing you could look in forever, even if it made your eyes feel sore and tired.

With Miss Agnes the world got bigger and then it got smaller. We used to think we were something, but then she told us all the things that were bigger than us, the universe and all that, and then all the things that were smaller. Too small to even see. So people were sort of in between, not big or small, just in between. That was a really interesting thing to think about.

Jimmy Sam brought in something every day to look at under the microscope. Miss Agnes told him there were much stronger microscopes that could see things even smaller than we could see with our microscope. Jimmy looked really surprised. "Where do they have those microscopes?" he asked.

Miss Agnes told him that he could go to college in Fairbanks and study with those powerful microscopes. Jimmy looked like he didn't really believe that, and I didn't really, either. People from our village don't go to college.

Miss Agnes got kind of mad when we all looked at her like that.

Just because he lived in a village all his life didn't mean he couldn't become a scientist, or anything else, she said. She started rattling off about this scientist or this artist or this writer who started out in a village like ours and went on to school. We were quite surprised, but Jimmy Sam was something different than surprised. His face was all red, and I could tell he'd made up his mind to do this microscope thing, right there when Miss Agnes was talking.

In a way we weren't surprised about Jimmy, how he started to think like that.

He was quiet, so quiet he could be there all day and never say anything unless you asked him a question. He had this way of looking at things very carefully, even little things. He was always taking things apart and putting them back together. Anything he was curious about. He was just a little kid, Grandpa said, when he took apart his dad's inboard motor. His dad got mad that time because he was ready to go to set the fishnet, and he had to wait for Jimmy to put his engine back together.

Jimmy was like that with other stuff, too. Once I saw him looking at a fern under the spruce tree by our school, and he looked at it for a long time, and then he began counting the little leaves. I asked him what he was doing, and he looked at me, surprised because he didn't know I was there.

"They come out just right," he said.

"What?" I said. I didn't know what he was talking about.

"Look," he said, "on each row there's just one

more leaf less, until it gets to the top. How does the fern know how to do this just right?"

I just goggled at him and shrugged.

I think that's why Jimmy didn't talk so much, because no one could figure out what he was talking about. Just Miss Agnes.

# Chapter 12

There was a record Miss Agnes used to play for us, from where she used to live in England. King's Choir, it was called. These people were singing in a big, big church made of stone, so their voices would echo like when we yell down at the bluff. When she played that record, she looked faraway again. We could see she was homesick for that place.

"My father was a teacher there before he died," she told us.

"In a church?" we asked.

"No. At the college there. Cambridge."

"Did he teach kids like us?"

"No. He taught mathematics to older students, college students. This church is there, right next to where he taught. I used to go there to listen to them sing when I was a child."

She will be happy to be back in England.

After *Robin Hood,* Miss Agnes read us Greek myths. Boy, those were something. To think of all the mischief those old-time people could get up to, changing into trees and that.

We loved the monster ones, and we drew pictures of the Chimera and the Hydra and the three-headed dog. That was a good one. And after that she read us the story about Ulysses, and that had more monsters. There was this one with just one big eye. I forget what you call him.

After that she read us all the fairy tales in the big red book. Those were kind of like the stories Old Miss Toby and Grandma would tell us at night up at fish camp. Those old stories about raven and people who turn into animals and all that.

We told Miss Agnes about those stories, and after that Miss Agnes would read us a fairy tale and then we would tell her one of the old-time stories. Miss Toby told them in Indian, so they sounded different when you tried to tell them in English. Not so good, somehow.

But that was fun, those fairy tales. My best was "Snow White," and Bertha's, too. We liked to think about all those funny little men.

# Chapter 13

When it was Christmastime, we had a tree in the school.

Toby Joe and Plasker went out with Toby Joe's little dog team to cut down a tree as soon as it got light, and they found a really good one. But it was too cold that day, fifty below zero, and all the needles just fell off on the way home. Too brittle. It was just a little skeleton they brought back that day. We all had to laugh.

Next day Toby Joe and Plasker got another one, and they got it right near the school and carried it easy like to the school so it wouldn't fall apart. So that was okay.

After we thawed it out, we put popcorn strings

on it and little chains made of green and red paper. That tree looked just beautiful.

It was supposed to have candles on it, but Miss Agnes said that spruce was too dry, the needles just falling off with a little sprinkling sound when you walked by it. We might set it on fire if we put candles on it.

Miss Agnes showed us some Christmas pictures from other countries, and those Christmas trees were just fat. Different from our skinny little trees. Our little, skinny tree branches couldn't even hold a candle, I don't think.

Miss Agnes taught us a whole bunch of Christmas songs. Some we knew from the radio already. And we put on a play.

Everyone came back from the trapline at Christmas, before they went out beaver trapping, so all the kids got to be in the play.

Some people went to Allakaket for Christmas, so they could go to the church there. But the rest of the people came to hear us sing and put on our play.

We did that one about ghosts, where this old

man is really selfish but these ghosts come to show him how bad he's been and how everyone doesn't like him. "A Christmas Carol," it's called, which is funny, because it's not about singing.

One of the ghosts, Plasker, had to have chains, so we put some marten traps together, and he let them just clank along. And one of the ghosts had to moan, and that was Toby Joe. He was just scary when he did that. Kenny and Roger were ghosts, too. I wanted to be a ghost, but Miss Agnes said we didn't have enough girls to waste them being ghosts, so I had to be the nephew's wife. That wasn't as much fun as a ghost. Jimmy Sam was the nephew, and he had to wear this tall black hat that kept falling off.

Charlie-Boy was Tiny Tim, that little crippled boy, and he had to be carried on his dad's back, so that had to be Little Pete because he was the only one big enough to carry Charlie-Boy. Marie was Mrs. Cratchit, and she had this kind of hat that was like a lace doily on her head, and her hair up. Marie had more fun than anyone, and she wasn't scared a bit.

Selina and Bertha got to be the Cratchit children, saying all this stuff about the goose.

Old Miss Toby came to watch, and my mother said the words in Indian for her so she could tell what we were saying, and boy, she really liked that play. In the Indian way the worst thing you could be is selfish, and everyone says if you do that, it will come back on you.

So Miss Toby thought that was a good play we did.

We made a lot of cookies and things for after the play, and Miss Agnes made a hot drink with apple juice and sugar and cinnamon in it to have with the cookies we made.

Miss Agnes took pictures of everyone after the Christmas play. First she took us all together, and then she took a picture of everyone just alone.

She had a camera with a bright light that flashed when she clicked the shutter. Everyone carried on and pretended that light made them blind and they couldn't see anything.

When we were eating the cookies and drinking the apple drink, Grandpa told us the story about when a priest came to Allakaket, when he was a little boy, and wanted to take a picture of everyone. No one had ever seen a camera before. The camera had a really bright flash, much bigger than the one on Miss Agnes's camera. It scared all the people so bad, everyone ran out of the church screaming.

We really laughed about that.

A while after everyone was back from beaver trapping, Miss Agnes showed us those pictures she took. She put a white sheet up on the wall, over all our drawings and the time line. It had to be dark in the room, so we blew out all the lamps, and then she put the little, square pictures in a machine and they blew up real big. Just like being in the picture, the pictures were so big.

We stared and stared. We never saw any pictures of ourselves before. We didn't look like what we thought. Toby Joe said, "Jeez, I look just like my brother!" That was funny because Toby Joe always called his brother "Ugly." Marie was happy to see herself up there. She looked beautiful, and you could tell she thought so, too.

I didn't even know myself in the pictures, but there was this girl wearing my sweater, so it had to be me. My hair was very messy, just like Mamma always tells me.

And my smile didn't look in the pictures the way it feels on my face. My smile looked like Bokko's smile, like our daddy's smile. I never knew that before.

Then Miss Agnes showed pictures of the places she'd been. The best ones were the pictures of Greece, where the Greek gods come from. There were all these old, white stone places partly knocked down. Temples and stuff.

There was England, and where she came from, the town where those people sang in the big church.

It was flat there, no hills, and we laughed at the river, it was so little and lazy. Just a creek, really. There were lots of guys rowing this one skinny boat, all bent forward at the same time.

There were flowers on the trees.

"That's how it is in springtime. Just about now," she said.

We were surprised, because it was still winter here. Forty below zero at night sometimes, though it got warm fast in the day because the sun was staying out a long time now. To think there were flowers somewhere right now, while we were here in the snow.

"Those flowers smell wonderful," she said. We could see how she could miss a place that had pink flowers on the trees. I would like to see that.

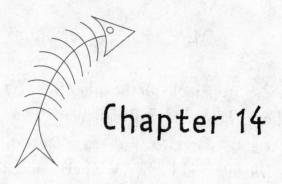

# Chapter 14

**Some** of the kids could read pretty good. Toby Joe was the best of us younger ones, because he would go to Old Man Andreson's and read all the magazines and stuff. And Jimmy Sam could read as good as Miss Agnes, really.

But Marie could hardly read at all, and none of us younger ones were much good at it. We read real slow, and the big words gave us fits. Selina and Charlie-Boy were still learning the alphabet.

Miss Agnes gave Jimmy and Toby Joe regular books to read, like *Tom Sawyer* and *Huckleberry Finn*. They just had to practice to get faster, she said.

For the rest of us Miss Agnes did something different.

We had these little books all the other teachers used, with Dick, Jane, and Sally in them. They had a mother and a father, and that's what they called them, Mother and Father. We never heard that before.

And there was a kitten named Puff and a dog named Spot. A little brown-and-white dog, low to the ground, with floppy ears.

They lived in a town with lots of trees along a cement road, and the houses were really big. All they did was play, those kids. The boy had short pants on, and the girl had yellow hair. And a ribbon in the hair. I think those kids were flesh colored, like the crayon.

When you read those books, it was kind of embarrassing. "Look, look, look. See Spot run." They talked kind of stupid like that.

So Miss Agnes didn't want us to read those books, but Marie, she liked them. She liked to look at the pictures, and Bertha and me did, too.

I liked to think about living in a place like

that, where everything was so clean and fancy. And they had a bedroom all for themselves, those kids.

I would like to have a mother like that, too, always smiling and making something good to eat. Milk and cookies, she always gave them. Well, I don't like milk, but the cookies would be very nice.

So Miss Agnes put those books away, and she made some other little books for us to read. A different one for each of us. Just little pieces of paper stapled together, but the thing about those books was they were about us. My book said this: "There once was a little girl named Fred. Her real name was Frederika, and she lived on the Koyukuk River with her mother, Anna, and her sister, Bokko." And there was more about me and Bokko playing and stuff, and our grandma, and what we did for work, like washing the dishes and bringing in the wood.

It was so good, I read it over and over, and that's how I learned those words.

Then every few days Miss Agnes would write

me another book with those words in them, and more, harder words.

She wrote one for Marie about how she'd grow up and get married and have a whole bunch of kids and how she would cook, and all that. Marie loved her book. When she read it, she'd get sort of pink in her cheeks, and you could see that Miss Agnes had written for her a life she wanted to have. Even if she had to take care of her mamma's kids so much, she wanted some of her own. She was just like that.

Pretty soon we were reading each other's books, and then we'd tell Miss Agnes what to put in each book for everyone. She'd write down the things we said.

And that's how we got along in our reading. Miss Agnes would make these little books for us, and when we knew them by heart, she'd give us new ones. It was easier learning to read that way. Seemed like none of the words never were hard that way.

And then she'd make us write stories, because she said that writing was just reading backwards, and you learned to read by writing just as well as reading. Reading backwards. We thought that was very funny.

Miss Agnes said not to worry about the spelling, just write. Anything we wanted to. Even we could make up stuff. It didn't have to be true. I really liked that. To make up pretend stories.

She gave each of us a little notebook. Any word we needed for our story she would write for us in that notebook. That was our own little dictionary. And that's the way we learned to spell.

Bokko would tell her story with signs to Miss Agnes, and she would write it on paper for her.

And so we'd do that every day, and then we'd read our stories out loud to the rest of the kids. Some of them were pretty funny.

Marie wrote one about getting her long hair caught in the wringer on the washing machine, and how her head was already pulled up to the place the clothes squeeze through before she got the washer shut off. Little Pete wrote about the time a mamma moose chased him up a tree when he was at fish camp because she thought he might hurt her baby.

I liked to write all the stuff Grandpa told me about the old days, and once I wrote all about Old Man Andreson's life. He had a lot of interesting things happen to him. I asked him a lot of questions and put the answers in my story, and he was just proud of that. Best of all, I liked to write about sort of magic things, like in the fairy stories. Magic snowshoes that would take you anywhere, and pills you could take to learn everything without even studying it. Stuff like that.

Writing stories was what I was good at. Miss Agnes said everyone was good at something, and when we asked her to tell us what we were good at, that's what she told me.

Charlie-Boy was good at sign language, and Jimmy was good at science. Selina was good at drawing, and Roger was good at airplanes. Kenny was good at music, and Bertha was good at printing and cursive. Little Pete was good at making people feel happy, and Marie was good at running the house and dancing.

Plasker was good at geography, Toby Joe was

good at reading, and Bokko was good at sewing.

When she got to me, she said, "Fred notices everything about everyone, what they say and do and look like. And what they're feeling. So she's good at writing stories."

We were all happy to hear what we were good at. I couldn't wait to tell Grandpa what she said about me. I was just proud.

# Chapter 15

**We** knew that we didn't talk the right way, because the other teachers had told us we had terrible English.

But Miss Agnes said there were lots of right ways to talk.

What we talked in the village was right, she said. That's the way to talk here. And when we talk in Athabascan, that's the right way, too. But there's another way to talk, and that's what we want to talk when we go to the city or go away to school, and that's what she said she was going to teach us.

So we learned that when we're somewhere else, we shouldn't say *ain't,* and we shouldn't mix up our *e*'s and *i*'s, like say *pin* when we mean *pen*. That's really hard to do.

We shouldn't say *gots* instead of *has*. You have to say *did*, like "He did it," not "He done it." And you can't say "I seen a moose." "I have seen a moose." That's the right way. Or "I saw a moose."

And then there's the thing about nothing words. That is really hard to get straight. If you use too many words that mean nothing, then it means something. Instead of nothing. Like if you say "I don't want nothing," then you mean you want *something*, because you said nothing wasn't what you wanted. So you say "I don't want anything." Whew.

The thing about good English is that when you say it right, it sounds wrong, because we're not used to saying it right. Miss Agnes said it takes practice.

Jimmy Sam looked at Miss Agnes and smiled that smile of his, like when she told him about the stars and all that. He was really happy with this good English he was learning. He liked to do things right.

After we studied English for a while, we made up this Good English game. Every time we caught somebody saying *ain't*, or using too many nothing words, or anything like that, we had to say, "Gotcha!" Then we could put a check mark by their name on the board. Whoever had the littlest check marks was the winner for that day.

I was the winner in that game lots, but it seemed like I had to think over every word I said before I said it.

After Christmas, Little Pete and Roger and the other kids were in school for a little while before they went out beaver trapping. That's when Miss Agnes read *The Adventures of Sherlock Holmes* to us, and *Kidnapped* and a book about King Arthur. She knew those big boys would like those ones. All of us did, they were so exciting.

In February, when everyone was back from beaver trapping, Miss Agnes read the story of Hudson Stuck to us. That's the one that was a priest. He used to travel all around here with a dog team, and he built the school at Allakaket and the mission and told all the people from all around to move there.

That was really interesting. There were lots of people in it who we knew. The old people were right in that book, *Ten Thousand Miles with a Dog Sled.* Even my grandpa. It made us feel like something, that someone had written this book about us, that we were in a book.

But the part Miss Agnes liked was about the boy the priest took with him. He was an Indian boy who didn't speak any English, and every night when they camped in their tent, even if it was fifty below zero, the priest would teach that boy, and after a while he was so smart he was going to go Outside to get to be a doctor. Hudson Stuck was sending him out to school to do that. To be the first Indian doctor.

But the boy was in a boat that hit an iceberg, and he and his new wife died in that cold water. So he never became a doctor.

Before Miss Agnes came, we didn't know people like us could learn that much and could be a doctor. It was in my head then, that I could do something really big. I didn't want to have babies, like Marie, and marry some boy. Maybe he'd get mean sometimes. Or have another girlfriend, like Martha's husband. I wouldn't like that.

I could make my own money. Sally Oldman went to Tanana when she was sixteen, and she worked there, helping the doctors. She didn't want no bunch of kids, either. Any.

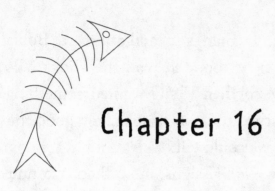

# Chapter 16

By spring we could all read pretty good and write stories and tell the names of the places on the whole map.

That big map was one of our best things. Plasker liked it the best. Plasker used to like to touch the map and say the names, low, like magic words. Like he could feel something coming from the countries on that map. I could do it, too, sometimes.

When I touched Africa, I could see that long, flat place where the elephants and the zebras were and feel the hot wind on me and smell dry grass. Now I wanted to go everywhere. And before, I never knew there was an everywhere.

By spring I could add and subtract. Bokko could write now, too, and read the books Miss Agnes wrote for her. If she wanted something, she could write to us now, not really good, but enough that we could tell.

She knew a lot of signs, more than two hundred, Miss Agnes said. And so did all of us. We learned right along with Bokko.

Only Miss Agnes had to look the signs up in the book all the time. She couldn't remember them as good as us. Sometimes she'd just ask us what the sign was for *book,* or *walk,* or something, and we'd tell her, so she wouldn't have to look it up. *"I have an old brain,"* she'd sign to Bokko. *"It's not good. A young brain is good."*

Even sometimes Bokko would sign bad things at us now, like when she got mad at us. Being mad in sign language is funny, so we'd laugh, and then Bokko would have to laugh, too.

The funny thing was that we didn't just use the signs to talk to Bokko, we used them to talk to each other. Like if Little Pete said something, maybe Roger would sign to him, *"You're crazy!"* or maybe when I saw Bertha in the store, I would just sign to her, *"Hi!"*

Pretty soon a lot of the grown-ups were learning some signs, too. Sometimes the old men sitting around in the store with Old Man Andreson would be funny, throwing their hands around, pretending they were talking real fast in sign language, to tease us.

When Mamma saw everyone getting interested in it, she even started to learn some signs. She would ask me how to say things like *be careful* and *hurry up* and bossy things like that, but me and Bokko didn't care, we were just happy she was learning and not mad about it anymore. And even sometimes Mamma would forget and would sign to me just like I was deaf, too. The first time it happened we all laughed, even Mamma, it was so funny.

By the time the snow had a hard crust from the warm days, it was time for nearly everyone to go to spring camp. Little Pete and Roger went to Long Lake. Marie and Plasker and Toby Joe went with their folks to North Fork, and Bertha went to spring camp up by Allakaket.

There were just five of us left in school. Charlie-Boy and Selina and me and Bokko and Kenny were staying in town until time for fish camp in the summer.

Spring camp was the best of all, really. Grandpa and Grandma and me and Mamma and Bokko went with Uncle Paddy and his family once, and it was so good.

We had two white tents we put up by the lake. In ours there were two bunks made from spruce poles, and there was a table and two gas boxes for chairs.

Uncle Paddy shoveled the snow over the edges of the tents to keep them tight, and set up a little Yukon stove in each tent. Those stoves kept the tents just warm.

When the ice on the lake melted, Grandpa and Uncle Paddy and the boys would go out in the little canoes and get as many muskrats as they could. Then at night all the grown-ups would skin and stretch the muskrats. When they were skinning, Grandpa told us stories about the old days, when he went for muskrats with his dad.

They used to make a tent with moose hides, put over willows bent in a bow. They had hard times those years, with no stores. Sometimes they were very hungry in the spring.

But this year the kids who were going to spring camp were sad. They knew when they got back Miss Agnes would be gone. It would all be over. There would be another teacher next year. Maybe a nice one, even. But never the same as Miss Agnes. What if she wouldn't let Bokko come to school?

When we talked like that, Miss Agnes would try to make us like the way things would be.

"Bokko will go to school," said Miss Agnes. "The priest at Allakaket said the church is going to send her to a good school for the deaf. When she's fourteen. It will be good. You'll see."

So Miss Agnes would be gone, and Bokko would be gone. Sometimes I went in the outhouse and I cried hard about that.

Maybe if one of us was smart like that boy of

Hudson Stuck's, the one who was going to be a doctor. Maybe if we didn't always have that fish smell on us. I know she said she couldn't even smell anything, but maybe. Maybe she would stay for us and teach us another year. Maybe if this England didn't have trees with pink flowers on them and that place where people sing so hard it bounces off the walls.

The days were so warm the ice on the river got rotten and we couldn't walk on it. Everything sounds louder when the snow is melting, and you can hear noises from a long way off, like the sound of someone chopping wood at the other end of the village.

Then the ice upriver started to push the ice by our village, and pretty soon that ice was breaking up into smaller pieces and moving down to the Yukon. The ice crunched and smashed along, pieces bumping into each other, noisy.

When the ice went out, it was almost the end of school and we were all getting ready to go to fish camp.

Miss Agnes packed her things. She didn't pack the books or the phonograph or the records. "I leave these for you," she said. "For next year. You tell the new teacher where the old books are. She'll likely want to use them."

She started to take the map and the pictures off the wall, but when she turned around, we were just staring at her. It seemed like we'd die if she took those things down. So she looked at us and then dusted her hands together the way she always did when she was making up her mind. She didn't take anything off the walls.

"We'll leave it just this way," she said.

I helped her some after everyone else had said good-bye and gone. When she had everything packed, she said to me, "This teapot is for you. Remember the first day I came, when you and Bertha had tea with me? This is to remember me by."

"Miss Agnes," I said. "I don't need nothing to remember you by. *Any*thing," I said, before she could correct me. "I will always remember you."

"Yes," she said. "Being a teacher is like that. No one ever forgets their teachers."

"What will you do when you get to England?"
I asked.

"The first thing is, I'll get into the subway and ride to Paddington Station." She smiled. "And then the train to Cambridge. And then . . . then I'll find a little house. And I'll live in it. And I'll go to King's Chapel. And have tea in a pub."

Her face was sad, and happy, too. I didn't want to look at her face anymore because I was going to cry, the kind of crying that makes your nose run and your throat ache.

"I have to go," I said. "Mamma is waiting for me."

"Yes," she said. "Take good care of Bokko, will you?"

"I will," I said.

# Chapter 17

**We** got back from fish camp late in September.

It was really fun to be there, but I missed Miss Agnes. Since she wouldn't be our teacher anymore, I wished we could just stay at fish camp all winter, too. Then we wouldn't have to get used to another new teacher.

At camp all my cousins from Nulato were there, and the aunts and my uncle Paddy. Bokko taught everyone her sign language. It was the first time she talked to all those people. She wasn't afraid anymore, or shy like she used to be. They were all happy to see Bokko so easy like now.

And they all bragged about Mamma when she talked to Bokko with signs, like she was the one who invented sign language. I think that made Mamma feel good, because she was nicer to everyone that summer and not so bossy.

We had hard work there at fish camp, just like every year. Uncle Paddy and his big boys would put the fish wheel in the river, and then they'd go out every morning in the boat to get the salmon out of the box.

My aunties and Mamma would cut the fish in strips, and then they'd drop it into the big tub full of salt water. Bokko and me would take it out of the salt water and carry it to the fish racks to hang up to dry.

It was really hard carrying that slippery, slimy fish just out of the salt water, and if we dropped it in the dirt, our aunties would just yell at us.

But we got a lot of fish, maybe more than any year. This year I wrote down the fish every day on the calendar. At the end of the week Bokko and I would add up all those fish.

Bokko and me were the only ones who could add those three numbers across. The grown-ups were proud of us. Mamma didn't say anything, and she tried to act like she knew all along we could do that adding, but I knew she was proud of us, too. We could tell she didn't think school was a waste of time anymore.

It seemed like everything reminded me and Bokko of Miss Agnes. Everything had something to do with what we learned from her, as if we just woke up to see the world around us, and way beyond us.

But when we thought about the things she taught us we thought about her not being there anymore. There was a lump in my throat every time I thought of that. I thought how we'd go to England to see her, but I knew I was just telling myself a story.

But maybe we'd always look for that to happen, the way people think something better is always going to happen to them someday.

It is late at night when we get home from fish camp. It is raining, dark and gloomy. No lights anywhere. Even Old Man Andreson must be asleep. No one knows we're coming.

Grandpa ties the boat and jams a pole in the mud to hold the boat away from the bank so it doesn't swamp. I have to carry the cooking stuff we're bringing home. It clanks away in an old burlap bag, knocking against my leg. Bokko is carrying another burlap bag with our radio in it, all wrapped up in a piece of tarp.

When we come around the corner, we see a light in the school. Someone has a lamp there. The new teacher.

Bokko and I stop to look. I feel terrible, and Bokko does, too, I can tell. We can't stop ourselves, though. We got to look. I put my bag down and walk softly up to the school window.

Bokko's behind me. We look in, but there's nothing to see. The room is the same, only darker than it was. Only one lamp burning.

Then we see there's a yellow cat sitting on the table, licking one paw. His eyes are closed, and he's licking that paw slowly, slowly. Bokko pulls in her breath sharply. We've never seen a cat, just in pictures. It's so pretty.

Then someone comes out of the darkness to shoo that cat off the table.

And it's Miss Agnes. Her hair is different somehow, but there are the pants. The cat jumps off the table, and Miss Agnes stops to scold him. And then I hear the music. That King's Choir. Bokko is crying, like she could hear it, too. Tears are running down her face.

We stand in the rain and look at Miss Agnes until she moves out of the window and into the back where we can't see her.

And then we go home. School will start at nine and we want to get a good night's sleep.

I'll ask her tomorrow why she came back to us.

# About the Author

**Kirkpatrick Hill** was raised in Fairbanks, Alaska. She graduated from Syracuse University with majors in English and education, and for the past thirty years has been an elementary-school teacher, spending most of her time in one-room schoolhouses in the Alaskan "bush." Her two previous books, *Toughboy and Sister* and *Winter Camp*, also take place in the Alaskan wilderness and have been immensely popular both in the United States and abroad.